A Richard Jackson Book

ORCHARD BOOKS · NEW YORK & LONDON

A division of Franklin Watts, Inc.

Great-uncle Felix

DENYS CAZET

Orchard Books, 387 Park Avenue South, New York, New York 10016
Orchard Books Great Britain, 10 Golden Square, London W1R 3AF England
Orchard Books Australia, 14 Mars Road, Lane Cove, New South Wales 2066
Orchard Books Canada, 20 Torbay Road, Markham, Ontario 23P 1G6

Orchard Books is a division of Franklin Watts, Inc.

Manufactured in the United States of America. Book design by Mina Greenstein.
10 9 8 7 6 5 4 3 2 1
The text of this book is set in 16 pt. Kennerley. The illustrations are pencil and watercolor drawings, reproduced in halftone.

Library of Congress Cataloging-in-Publication Data: Cazet, Denys. Great-uncle Felix.   Summary: A young boy learns self-confidence, love, and the value of memory from his great-uncle.   [1. Uncles—Fiction. 2. Self-confidence—Fiction] I. Title. PZ7.C2985Gr 1988   {E}   87-24682
ISBN 0-531-05750-X   ISBN 0-531-08350-0 (lib. bdg.)

E
C

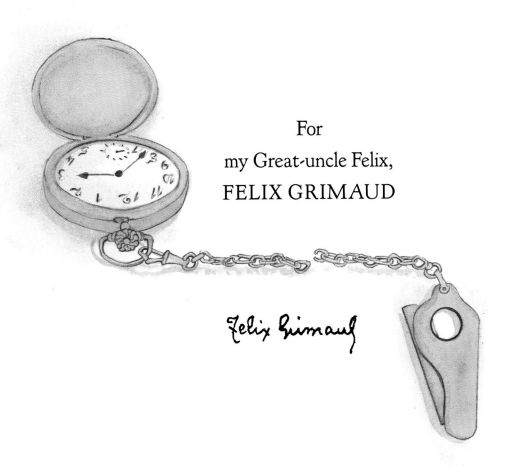

For
my Great-uncle Felix,
FELIX GRIMAUD

Felix Grimaud

*G*reat-uncle Felix stepped off the bus.

He tipped his hat at two passing ladies and looked for Sam.

"Here I am, Uncle Felix," Sam shouted. "Over here."

Great-uncle Felix gave Sam a rhinoceros hug.

"I knew you would be here to meet me."

"I got here early," said Sam, "just in case. Mom and Dad are getting your room specialed."

Sam lifted Uncle Felix's heavy suitcase onto his bicycle. "This is my Great-uncle-Felix's-suitcase holder. I made it myself."

Suddenly, the suitcase fell to the sidewalk.
"Needs work," said Sam.

"I think it's a marvelous invention," said Great-uncle Felix.
Sam nodded. "Sort of…"
They fastened the suitcase back on the bicycle.

Uncle Felix reached into his pocket.

"See this, Sam?" he said. "This champion yo-yo belonged to your mother."

He twirled the yo-yo. He did three loop-the-loops in a row.

Sam tried one.

The yo-yo flew past Great-uncle Felix and landed in the water.

"I guess I need a little practice," Sam said.

"Plenty of time," said Great-uncle Felix.

Suddenly, the bicycle rack collapsed.

"I'll take care of the bicycle," Uncle Felix told Sam, "and you rescue the yo-yo."

Great-uncle Felix picked up his suitcase.

Sam fished the yo-yo out of the lake.

"Wow!" said Sam. "This is a Triple-Star-Flyer. It looks brand new."

"I found it in the window seat," said Great-uncle Felix, "when I was cleaning up a bit."

"I know," said Sam. "By the window in the dining room.
When the sun shined through the lace curtains, Aunt Rose's
canaries sang and sang."

"I'm surprised you remember that," Uncle Felix said.

"I remember," said Sam.

Great-uncle Felix looked out across the lake.

"I remember," he said, "when your Great-aunt Rose and I used to sail our boat on this lake. Just the two of us. Under this very same sky."

"I remember something else," said Sam.

"I remember she kept extra peppermints in her purse,"
said Sam.

They crossed the street and stopped in front of Sam's house.

Suddenly, the suitcase sprang from the bicycle and bounced onto the lawn.

"We're home!" shouted Great-uncle Felix.

"Just in time," Sam muttered.

"What's the matter?"

"I can't do anything right," said Sam. "I wanted to do something for you that nobody else could do. Just me."

Great-uncle Felix sat down next to Sam. "You already have! Why, if it wasn't for you, I'd be just a ho-hum uncle. Not a king. Not a prince. Just an ordinary, ho-hum uncle. You put the *great* in Great-uncle Felix."

"I did all that?" said Sam. "I don't remember."

"Well, you were *very* small."

Sam smiled. "Great-uncle Felix?"

"Yes, great nephew Sam?"

"Would you help me untangle the yo-yo?"

83513

Cazet...Great-Uncle Felix.

WITHDRAWN